To my father and brother,

who traveled to the end of the world to find what matters most.

MARIA VAN LIESHOUT

Hopper and Wilson

Philomel Books

An Imprint of Penguin Group (USA) Inc.

opper and Wilson looked out
over the big blue sea.
And wondered.

"What," Hopper asked his little
friend Wilson, "do you think it's
like at the end of the world?"

"Not sure, Hopper," Wilson answered,
"but I bet there's lots of lemonade!
I love lemonade."

"And a staircase to the
moon!" Hopper said.
"So I can touch it."

"Well, there's only one way to find out," Hopper said.
They packed their balloon with the red string, launched
their boat, and said good-bye to their cactus.

"You can't come
along," Wilson peeped.
"You're too small."

And off they sailed.

They waved until their
cactus had disappeared behind
the edge of the sea.

They bobbed on the waves and dreamed about
what they would find at the end of the world.

When a star dashed across the sky, the two friends closed their
eyes and made a wish. Hopper wished to touch the moon.
Wilson hoped to find an endless supply of lemonade.

They woke up when fat
drops of rain hit their faces.

"I hope our journey
won't be too choppy," Hopper said.

"I wish we'd brought a blanket,"
Wilson said, shivering.

The breeze turned into gusts. Gusts became howling winds that flung the boat from wave to wave.

"HOLD ON, HOPPER!"

But the sea was loud and angry, and it swallowed up Wilson's scream.

Hopper couldn't hear a thing except the roar of the crashing waves.

When the sea settled down and the wind grew silent,
Hopper wasn't in the boat anymore.

Wilson was afraid.

He looked for Hopper among the sea turtles.

"I lost my friend Hopper. Have you seen him by chance?"

They had not.

On the icebergs . . .

"He's a big guy.
Funny ears."

Wilson even asked a giant fish.
"Hopper is not good at being alone,
you see . . ."

But the fish just blinked and swam away.

When Wilson looked up, he saw a bird
carrying their balloon's red string.

He gasped, "Do you know where Hopper is?"

The bird circled above the boat and then flew into the fog.

So Wilson sailed into the fog too.

"Hopper?"

"HOPPER!!!"

"Wilson, is that you?"
called a voice.

"Wilson!"

"Hopper!"

Hopper and Wilson held each other for a long time.

"I missed you, Wilson."   "I missed you too, Hopper."

That's when something peeked over the edge of the sea.
The two friends cheered and laughed and danced.
"We've arrived at the end of the world!"

"I bet I can reach the moon
from there," Hopper said.

"Are those lemons?"
Wilson asked.

"And there is our cactus! We're home!" Wilson peeped.

"Aren't we lucky that our home is at
the end of the world, Wilson?"

Wilson closed his eyes.
"And at the beginning too!" he peeped.

PHILOMEL BOOKS
A division of Penguin Young Readers Group. Published by The Penguin Group.
Penguin Group (USA) Inc., 375 Hudson Street, New York, NY 10014, U.S.A.
Penguin Group (Canada), 90 Eglinton Avenue East, Suite 700, Toronto, Ontario M4P 2Y3, Canada
(a division of Pearson Penguin Canada Inc.).
Penguin Books Ltd, 80 Strand, London WC2R 0RL, England.
Penguin Ireland, 25 St. Stephen's Green, Dublin 2, Ireland (a division of Penguin Books Ltd).
Penguin Group (Australia), 250 Camberwell Road, Camberwell, Victoria 3124, Australia (a division of Pearson Australia Group Pty Ltd).
Penguin Books India Pvt Ltd, 11 Community Centre, Panchsheel Park, New Delhi - 110 017, India.
Penguin Group (NZ), 67 Apollo Drive, Rosedale, North Shore 0632, New Zealand (a division of Pearson New Zealand Ltd).
Penguin Books (South Africa) (Pty) Ltd, 24 Sturdee Avenue, Rosebank, Johannesburg 2196, South Africa.
Penguin Books Ltd, Registered Offices: 80 Strand, London WC2R 0RL, England.

Design by Semadar Megged.   Text set in 17-point Goudy Catalogue MT.
The art was created with watercolors, ink, collage, colored pencil, crayon, a smudge of acrylics and some technology to pull it all together.
Library of Congress Cataloging-in-Publication Data
Van Lieshout, Maria.   Hopper and Wilson / by Maria van Lieshout.   p. cm.
Summary: An elephant and a mouse embark on a journey to discover what it looks like at the end of the world.
[1. Sailing—Fiction. 2. Elephants—Fiction. 3. Mice—Fiction.] I. Title. PZ7.V2753Ho 2011 [E]—dc22 2010019396
ISBN 978-0-399-25184-9
1 3 5 7 9 10 8 6 4 2